V/06

W9-CQL-216

SHEEP DREAMS

by Arthur A. Levine

pictures by Judy Lanfredi

Dial Books for Young Readers New York

Published by Dial Books for Young Readers
A Division of Penguin Books USA Inc.
375 Hudson Street
New York, New York 10014

Printed in Hong Kong
by South China Printing Company (1988) Limited
Design by Amelia Lau Carling
First Edition
1 3 5 7 9 10 8 6 4 2

Library of Congress Cataloging in Publication Data
Levine, Arthur A., 1962–
Sheep dreams | by Arthur A. Levine ; pictures by Judy Lanfredi.
p. cm.
Summary: Although Liza, a young sheep, dreams of being
a star, she is too shy to try out for the lead
in the class play—but a crisis on opening night
thrusts her into the spotlight.
ISBN 0-8037-1194-8 (trade).—ISBN 0-8037-1195-6 (lib. bdg.)
[1. Sheep—Fiction. 2. Bashfulness—Fiction.
3. Plays—Fiction.] I. Lanfredi, Judy, ill. II. Title.
PZ7.L57824Sh 1993 [E]—dc20 91-44929 CIP AC

The art for each picture was prepared using black
pencil, black ink, and watercolor. It was then color-separated
and reproduced as red, blue, yellow, and black halftones.

To Laurie, Cindy, Kate, and Jane
—my beloved little chillers
A.A.L.

To my parents, with love,
and to my yiayiá, Agathé
Μέ απέραντη ἀγάπη
J. L.

Liza Shetland dreamed big.
To get to sleep she counted movie stars decked out in shiny costumes, glittering with jewels—daring and glamorous.

And just as Liza drifted off, a spotlight would frame her,
alone on stage, singing her heart out at the top of her lungs....

But when she was awake, she barely said a word. She was too shy. Her dad always had to guess what she wanted for breakfast.

She *never* spoke up at school. Even when Cashmere LaFondue, the most popular girl in class, called out, "Who wants to play Actress with me at recess?" Liza didn't say, "ME! I want to." She double-checked her spelling words instead.

Then one day Ms. Hoofman announced auditions for the class musical. Liza wanted the part of Amelia Eweheart, the famous pilot, so badly that her nose twitched all the way home. She was determined to sing out when the time came.

All that week Liza practiced. She chirped with the birds at the crack of dawn.

She howled with the Hound Dogs down the road.

She belted out encore after encore in front of her mirror.
The applause was deafening.

When audition day came, Liza was ready. She wore her lucky purple bow to school. And at lunch she ate only an apple to keep her throat clear.

But when she walked into the audition room, she saw
Cashmere LaFondue tap dancing on the piano, tossing off easy
high notes and dazzling everyone. She was just too cool.
Liza slunk to the back of the line for nonspeaking parts.

So Cashmere got the part of Amelia, and all the great solos. Liza was stuck with the group of fans throwing confetti during Amelia's landing. She didn't even get to hum.

Liza's parents tried to be helpful. They set up chairs in the living room and got Liza to sing the solos just for them. Then they clapped loudly. That felt a little better.

But it wasn't enough. By the night of the show, Liza wished she didn't have to go. She took forever getting ready and almost forgot to bring her confetti.

When they finally got to school, the auditorium was packed full. Liza had to say, "Excuse me, exCUSE me" four times to get to the stage.

The moment Liza stepped behind the curtain, Ms. Hoofman grabbed her. "Liza, have you seen Cashmere?" she wailed. "The curtain's about to go up!"

Liza shrugged her shoulders. Then she went to find the darkest corner to hide in until the play began.

But someone had gotten there first: Cashmere LaFondue!
And she was shaking like lime jello on a motorcycle.
"L-L-Liza, you've got to help me," she stammered.

Liza couldn't believe it. Cashmere? Scared?

"Liza, I can't go out there. My p-p-parents are in the
audience."

A few yards away Ms. Hoofman was still looking for
Cashmere. "Check the Girls' Room!" she shouted at Fifi Fanelli.
"Check the supply closet!" she ordered Morty, the janitor.

But it was too late. The piano player had begun the first number. Ms. Hoofman's eyes bugged out. She screamed, "Hold this!" at Morty, and ran off. So there he was with Cashmere's costume when the curtain started to go up.

Liza leapt into action. She grabbed onto the bottom of the curtain, but it kept going up, leaving her hooves dangling a foot off the floor.

Morty tried to help her, but she wound up sitting on his shoulders as he swayed back and forth.

Just then Simon and Wendy, dressed as a camel, came trotting onto the stage and crashed into Liza and Morty. Everyone fell over in a heap.

For a moment the auditorium was silent as snow.
Then little Byron Bigglesworth, who had practiced his
two lines all week, shuffled onstage, concentrating with
all his might.

"Hey everyone, there's Amelia Eweheart, the famous pilot, back from one of her daring missions!" he said. "What was it like, Amelia?"

But he was pointing at *Liza!*

Liza could hear the crowd murmuring as the piano
started up again. All she could see was the glare of the
spotlights. Then her vision cleared and a sea of goggle-eyed
parents popped into focus. Liza knew it was up to her.
She opened her mouth, but nothing came out!

Then she spotted them. *Her* parents—holding hooves in the fourth row and smiling, just like in their living room. Liza blocked out everything else in the theater and swallowed hard. She took a deep breath, tossed back her scarf, and…

let out a bleat that beat the band.

By the finale everyone knew that the famous pilot was Liza.
Or rather that Liza was Amelia.

And Liza was a star!